My Book of Poems

Poems by Debbie Croft
Illustrations by Wayne Bryant

Contents

Crabs

We walked down to the beach one day,
Along a sandy track,
And stopped to look at rock pools,
That we found on our way back.

Near the pools we saw some crabs,
We watched them dart and play,
And rush into the water,
Running sideways all the way!

Others crawled between the rocks,
And some began to fight.
I think that they were looking
For somewhere to rest that night.

Some slept in cracks and small dark caves,
Where they were safe and cool,
But then they woke and had to catch
Their dinner in the pool!

Pets

It seems sometimes as though our dogs
Are cared for extra well.
For when we went on holidays,
They lived in a hotel!

We packed them in the car,
And dropped them off as we left town.
There were lots of other animals,
Some black, some white, some brown!

They very quickly made new friends,
They ran and played and scampered.
Then it was back inside again,
So they could all be pampered!

Their coats were washed.
Their nails were clipped.
Their dinner bowls all shone.
It only took two minutes
And then all the food was gone!

Some dogs tried to do new tricks,
Like how to fetch a ball,
Or how to jump through big round hoops,
And stand up proud and tall.

When we called to pick them up,
I think I heard one say,
"We don't mind staying here,
When is your next holiday?"

The Sun

Each day the sun comes peeping out,
Early in the morning.
It always comes up in the east,
As each new day is dawning.

It warms the Earth so new plants grow,
It gives off lots of light,
It slowly moves across the sky,
From morning until night.

Each night the sun goes far away,
It sets out in the west.
Everybody goes indoors,
And birds go to their nests.

While we are tucked up snug in bed,
The sun warms other places,
Until next morning, back it comes,
To shine on all our faces!

The Kiwi and the Emu

The kiwi and the emu
Are both birds that cannot fly.
They run but do not leave the ground,
No matter how they try.

The kiwi has no tail,
But it has feet with three big toes.
It has a bill that's very long,
With nostrils like our nose!

The kiwi lays just one large egg,
That may be green or white.
It's sometimes in a hollow log,
A safe place day and night.

The kiwi eats small worms and grubs,
Or insects, fruit and seeds.
It scratches on the ground at night,
To find the food it needs.

The emu is Australian,
It has feathers soft and brown.
It lives out in the country,
Or just outside the town.

It sometimes grows two metres tall,
Its legs and neck are long.
It runs a long way at top speed
Because its legs are strong.

The emu lays eggs in a nest,
The shells are strong and green.
These eggs are very large,
Perhaps the biggest that you've seen!

The kiwi and the emu
Are both birds that cannot fly,
I wonder what they think of birds
That soar across the sky?

Photographs

My grandad has some photographs,
From when he was a boy.
They show him riding on his horse
And playing with a toy.

My dad showed me some photographs,
From when he was a child.
They show him swimming in the sea,
With waves so high and wild.

I have a photograph of me,
From when I was just four.
There's Grandad and my dad,
With my new train set on the floor!

The Water Park

I carefully climbed to the top of the slide,
Waving at Dad and smiling so wide.
I waited my turn.

    "Here I go now!" I cried.
Splishing and splashing from side to side,
Down …

    down …

        down …
What a ride!